A Startright Elf

Baby Book

Baby's Songs

Illustrated by Cathy Beylon

Brown Watson

ENGLAND
Art and text copyright © 1988 Checkerboard Press, Inc.
All rights reserved.
Printed and bound in Belgium.
STARTRIGHT ELF and the Startright Elf logo are trademarks of
Checkerboard Press, Inc. USA. 0 9 8 7 6 5 4 3 2 1

ROCK-A-BYE, BABY

Rock-a-bye, baby, on the tree-top,
When the wind blows the cradle will rock.
When the bough breaks the cradle will fall,
And down will come baby, cradle and all.

TWO LITTLE DUCKS

Two little ducks that I once knew,
Fat ducks, skinny ducks, there were two.
But the one little duck with feathers on his back,
He led the other with a quack, quack, quack.

Down to the river they would go,
Wobble, wobble, wobble, wobble, to and fro.
But the one little duck with feathers on his back,
He led the other with a quack, quack, quack.

DOWN BY THE STATION

Down by the station early in the morning,
See the little puffer trains all in a row.

The man in the engine pulls a little lever,
Puff, Puff, toot! toot! Off we go.

BAA, BAA, BLACK SHEEP

Baa, baa, black sheep, have you any wool?
Yes sir, yes sir, three bags full.
One for my master, one for my dame,
One for the little boy who lives down the lane.

DING, DONG, BELL!

Ding, dong, bell!
Pussy's in the well!
Who put her in?
Little Johnny Thin.
Who pulled her out?
Little Johnny Stout.

What a naughty boy was that
To try to drown a pussy cat,
Which never did him any harm,
But killed all the mice in his father's barn!

POP! GOES THE WEASEL

All around the mulberry bush
The monkey chased the weasel.
The monkey thought 'twas all in fun,
Pop! goes the weasel!
A penny for a spool of thread,
A penny for a needle,
That's the way the money goes,
Pop! goes the weasel!

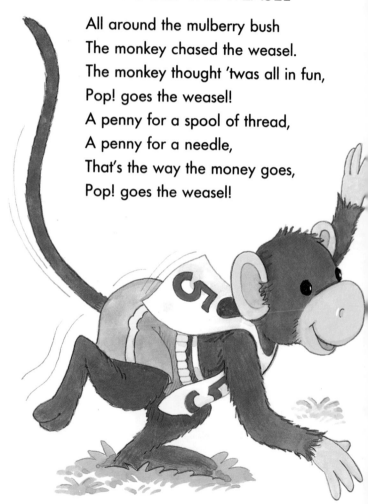

IT'S RAINING, IT'S POURING

It's raining, it's pouring,
The old man is snoring.
He bumped his head and he went to bed,
And he wouldn't get up in the morning.

EENSY WEENSY SPIDER

Eensy Weensy Spider climbed
 the water spout.
Down came the rain and
 washed the spider out.
Out came the sun and
 dried up all the rain.
So Eensy Weensy Spider
 climbed the spout again.

HICKORY, DICKORY, DOCK

Hickory, dickory, dock,
The mouse ran up the clock.

The clock struck one,
The mouse ran down!
Hickory, dickory, dock.

POLLY, PUT THE KETTLE ON

Polly, put the kettle on,
Polly, put the kettle on,
Polly, put the kettle on.
We'll all have tea.

Sukey, take it off again,
Sukey, take it off again,
Sukey, take it off again.
They've all gone away.

I SEE THE MOON

I see the moon,
The moon sees me.
God bless the moon,
And God bless me.

TWINKLE, TWINKLE, LITTLE STAR

Twinkle, twinkle, little star,
How I wonder what you are.
Up above the world so high,
Like a diamond in the sky,
Twinkle, twinkle, little star,
How I wonder what you are.

PRINTED IN BELGIUM BY
proost
INTERNATIONAL BOOK PRODUCTION